MINE!

Pictures

SHARON R

Words by

ALISON GREEN

For Gill Floyd

First published in the UK
in 2018 by Alison Green Books
An imprint of Scholastic Children's Books
Euston House, 24 Eversholt Street, London NW1 1DB
A division of Scholastic Ltd. www.scholastic.co.uk
London – New York – Toronto – Sydney – Auckland
Mexico City – New Delhi – Hong Kong
Copyright © 2018 Sharon Rentta
HB ISBN: 978 1 407171 81 4
PB ISBN: 978 1 407171 82 1
All rights reserved. Moral rights asserted.
Designed by Zoë Tucker
Printed in Malaysia
9 8 7 6 5 4 3 2 1
Papers used by Scholastic Children's Books are
made from wood grown in sustainable forests.

Down in the
forest . . .

creak . . .
Snap . . .

BUMP!

"Mine!"
says Good Wolf.

Wheeee!

Pat!

Jump!

But, elsewhere
in the forest . . .

kick . . .

shove . . .

Crack!

Bad Bird hatches.

Stomp,
stomp,
flap!

Bad Bird creeping,
    peeping, sees:

Good Wolf playing
underneath the trees.

"Ha!" says Bad Bird.
"I'll have that!"

Flip-flap-flutter

–shhhhh!

"Mine!"

Nab!

Grab!

"NA-na-na-NAH-NAHHH!
You can't catch ME!"

Sad Good Wolf thinks,

"Hmm. We'll see."

"Sing to me, Bad Bird.
You sing so well."

"La-da-di-da-DAAA!
Ding-dong-BELL!"

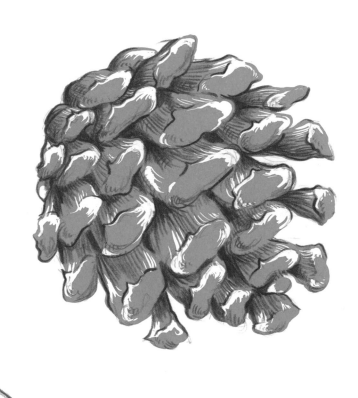

"Mine!"

crows Good Wolf.

"Mine!
Cheep!
CHIRP!"

"No, **mine!**" grins Good Wolf.

SNAP!

Yum,
yum,
burp!

Evening in the forest,
and . . . shhh!
What's that?

Good Wolf is playing still.

Wheeee! Jump! PAT!